Alfred Rochefort Calhoun

The Color Guard

Alfred Rochefort Calhoun

The Color Guard

ISBN/EAN: 9783337334727

Printed in Europe, USA, Canada, Australia, Japan

Cover: Foto ©Andreas Hilbeck / pixelio.de

More available books at **www.hansebooks.com**

dor Guard;

ARY DRAMA

IVE ACTS,

NYING TABL

PITTSBURGH:

. . . . & SONS, BOOK AND JOB PRINTERS, 67 AND 69 FIFTH AVENUE.

1870.

NOTICE.

CAST.

MR. LUDLOW.......... ....Village Banker
LOUIS LUDLOW.......... ....Afterward Color Bearer
JACKSON LUDLOW......... .... "   Color Guard
FARMER JOHNSON.
JACK JOHNSON....................... ....Afterward Color Guard
SAM ROBERTS.............. .... "   "   "
JIM HANSOM..... .. . . "   "   "
SQUIRE WILLIAMS....... ....School Trustee
MR. GRAY.. ....Citizen
POST MASTER.
ALFRED THORNTON..............................Afterward Capt. C. S. A.
TOM FLYNN... ....Irishman
BOB MASON.......................Tennesseean, afterward Union Scout
LONG GEORGE... ......Tennesseean
PETER HIGGLY.................................... ....Dutchman
MOUNTAINEER.
FATHER ALLEN..Refugee
REFUGEE.
LIEUT. OF GUERILLAS.
CAPTAIN C. S. A.
TONEY....... ....Servant to Captain Thornton
PRISONER.
SERGEANT U. S. A.
NEWS BOY.

LADY CHARACTERS.

LUCY JOHNSON,	ALICE GRAY,
JERUSHA JOHNSON,	SUSAN MARIA HANSOM,
ABBIE SMITH,	GODDESS OF LIBERTY.

    Ladies for Tableaux. Officers and Soldiers, Mountaineers, Refugees, Prisoners, Citizens, &c.

COSTUME.

MR. LUDLOW.—1st, Gentleman dress suit. 2d, Change at will.

LOUIS LUDLOW.—1st, Citizen's dress. 2d, Serg't U. S. Army. 3d, Capt. U. S. Army.

JACKSON LUDLOW.—1st, Citizen's dress. 2d, Private U. S. Army.

FARMER JOHNSON.—1st, Plain suit. 2d, Change at will.

JACK JOHNSON.—1st, Citizen's dress. 2d, Private U. S. Army.

SAM ROBERTS.—1st, Plain suit. 2d, Private U. S. Army.

SQUIRE WILLIAMS.—1st, Plain Citizen's dress. 2d, Change at will.

MR. GRAY.—1st, Neat home suit. 2d, Change at will.

ALFRED THORNTON.—1st, Stylish street dress. 2d, Capt. C. S. A.

TOM FLYNN.—1st, Shabby suit. 2d, Ragged uniform C. S. A. 3d, Plain Citizen's suit.

BOB MASON.—1st, Mountain dress. 2d, Ragged. 3d, Private U. S A. 4th, Plain old suit.

LONG GEORGE.—Mountain hunters costume.

PETER HIGGLY.—Plain Citizen's dress.

FATHER ALLEN.—Ragged dress.

TONEY.—1st, Plain grey dress. 2d, Neat Citizen's suit.

LUCY JOHNSON.—1st, Neat home suit. 2d, Street dress. 3d, Plain black. 4th, Change at will.

JERUSHA JOHNSON.—1st, Plain home suit. 2d, Street dress. 3d Change at will.

ABBIE SMITH.—1st, Neat servant's suit. 2d, Street dress. 3d Change at will.

ALICE GRAY.—1st, Neat home suit. 2d, Walking suit.

SUSAN MARIE HANSOM.—1st, Plain suit. 2d, Change at will.

THE COLOR GUARD.

ACT I.

SCENE FIRST.

Village street and post office. Squire Williams, Farmer Johnson and Citizens discovered waiting for the mail. Lively music.

Squire W.—Now let me say farmer Johnson, I don't think we're agoing to have any war. (*Business.*) My opinion is this, I'm a school trustee, and ought to know. The politicians and provision men have formed a combination to run up prices, so they've started this story about war. Now I'll bet my best heifer I'm right.

Farmer J.—Well I know you'r pretty long headed squire, but I differ for once with you. There's allus fire whar there's smoke. My Jack was over to Portsmouth yesterday, and he hurd it read out of a paper that the southern people had fired on the flag, some were's down south, and that Lincoln, him as you fellohs 'lected, had called for a whole lot of men. I did'nt vote for Lincoln, but by the fernal, I'll stand by the Union, and so will my boy. He aint old enough to vote, but he dared that sneak Alf Thornton to fight not long go, and I jest reckon he can lick any man of his years south of the Ohio. Them's my principles.

Squire W.—Now, Mr. Johnson, don't get excited. I stick to my opinion, and if there's to be war, I'll send in Jim Hansom, my son-in-law, if it makes Susan Maria a widder. But see the mail has just come in, let us see the Post master and borrow a paper.

Post Master at window.—Thunder and greased lightning, friends, we are in for it. (*Drops back.*)

[ENTER TOM FLYNN, 1ST L.]

Tom F.—Musha, listen to that fellow, what does he mane we're in for? If its a fight Tom Flynn's yer boy. I'll fight any man in the place for one dollar and fifty cents Gorra, but I'd make it a thousand if I had the money.

1*

[Enter Mr. Ludlow, 1st L.]

Mr. L.—Hello, Tom! Drunk again, are you?

Tom F.—Dhrunk! Well, Mr. Ludlow, a man of your sinse to call me dbrunk; sbure Tom's never drunk while he has a cint in his pocket, but barrin' yersel, Mr. Ludlow, gorra but I can whip any man in the place. (*Yells.*)

Mr. L.—(to *Postmaster*). You seem excited, Mr. McDonald. Anything for me to-day?

Postmaster.—Oh, Lud! Mr. Ludlow! We are ruined. The Union busted; the flag insulted, and the Devil to pay. Here, you have a big mail, one letter from the South. Reckon its from your brother, though I only read the post mark. Atlanta, Georgia.

(*Hands Mr. L. a bundle, Mr. L. glances hurriedly at a paper.*)

Squire W.—I don't get any papers, but if you'd loan me that what you'r reading, Mr. Ludlow, I'd be very much obliged.

Mr. L.—Certainly, Squire.

(*Hands paper, opens letter and reads.*)

Squire W.—Friend Johnson, I back down, I cave, I obsquatulate, it ain't the politicians and provision men. By the livin' thunder, it's the politicians alone. War. War. War. The papers covered with it. I know'd it was comin'. Didn't I allus say we'd have war. I'll bet my best heifer my Susan Maria is goin' to be a widder.

Farmer J.—You'r a heavy old prophet, Squire. You just take the shine out of Joe Young an' all the Mormons. Let me see the paper. (*Takes paper, reads and comments*). Lincoln has called for seventy-five thousand men. Lord, what a big pile. The States are to be divided. Not by the 'Tarnel, while me and my boy Jack's livin'. (*Reads*). See here, Squire! Why our Guvener calls for men. That's my stile. That's the way to show Ohio may vote as she choses; but by the 'Tarnel, Ohio stands by the Union.

Tom F.—To the Devil wid the Guvener. If yees want any fightin' done, jist sind for Tom Flynn. By Gorra the Flynn's were always in for a fight.

[Enter Jack Johnson, 2nd R., and lays hand on shoulder of Tom F.]

Jack J.—Well, Tom, what are you blowing about; do you want to fight, eh?

Tom F.—Fight! Is it me want to fight Mr. Jack? Arrah, show me the man that says so, and I ll put a mug on him his own darling mother wouldn't know. Not me, Mr. Jack. Come, take a dhrink;

one dollar and fifty cents to do it on. Gorra but we'll have a day of it. Come, Jack, agrab, wud me, yer bist friend, Tom Flynn.
                    (*Tries to pull Jack J. away.*)
Jack J.—Not now, Tom. The old man looks as if he wanted me.
                    (*Walks aside with Farmer J.*)

[ENTER 2D R., JACKSON LUDLOW.]

Jackson L.—Why father, are you sick? I never saw you looking so pale and excited. Come, let me take you home.
Mr. L.—No, my son, I am not unwell. But the news that comes to us to-day is most alarming. The South is in for war. Troops are called out by the Union, and you, my boy, must go, and Louis too.
Jackson L.—I am glad, father, you feel so, for I made up mind to enter the army yesterday, when Jack Johnson and I were in Portsmouth. But what is that letter you cling to so.
Mr. L.—It is from your Uncle Martin and your brother Thomas, who still remains with him. Let me read it. (*All gather round*).

[ENTER 2D R. ALF. THORNTON.

Mr. L.—(*Reads*).   ATLANTA, GA., April 18th, 1861.
My Dear Brother. By the time this reaches you you will have heard that the South has determined to sever a Union in which it can have no protection, and build up a Confederacy where there will be the most ample protection to all men in the stations which God called them to fill. We have struck the first blow at Charleston, and above the stars and stripes now floats the flag of the South. We hope to leave in peace, though amply prepared for war. We have plenty of friends North, and knowing your spirit of justice, I think I may count you among them. You will be pleased to learn that Thomas your son has enrolled his name in the Georgia State Guards. He sends love to all, and I with him hope to hear from you before the postal communications between the separate nations cease, which I presume will be a temporary necessity of Secession.
            Faithfully your brother,
                          MARTIN LUDLOW.

Squire W.—Jest as I said, them southern fellows is for war. But we'll give 'em Hail Columbia if Susan Maria lets her husband go. Him as is my son-in-law.
Jackson L.—Father, this is terrible. Poor Tom, he has been led blindly into this. But with your consent, I will fight for the Union, though every man with a drop of our blood in his veins opposes us.
Mr. L.—God bless you, my boy, I feel as you do.
Farmer J.—Here's my Jack. I'm an ole Democrat, one of them

as stands by the country, an' I'll send him in with your boys, Mr·
Ludlow, and I'll give up my farm if Uncle Sam wants it, an' more,
this ole arm can hold a rifle, and my eye aint too dim to guide a
bullet yet if need be.

Alfred T.—See here, friends, my opinion is, you are all too one-
sided. Across the Ohio river are our friends and relatives. North
of us is a land of mean skin-flints. I was born North but raised
South.

Jack J.—You mean you gambled South.

Tom F.—Let the gintlemin talk, the Flynns were always for lettin' a man talk.

Alf. T.—I know my own business. This is a free country and I
am not afraid to say if there is to be war, I will draw my sword for
the South.

Farmer J.—I knew you were a villian from the day you first came
to see my daughter, and if the people felt as I do they would hang
you on the spot.

All shout—Hang him. Hang the Rebel. (*Crowd seizes Alf. T.,
while one brings rope*).

[ENTER LOUIS LUDLOW, 2D R.]

Louis L.—Stand back here. This scene will do for the South,
but not for the law-abiding North. Jack and you, brother, help
me. (*Releases Alf. T.*) A man is ever at liberty to express his sentiments here without fear, no matter how much we despise him.
Here, sir, I will escort you from the crowd, and it is with the hope
that I may meet you some day better prepared to defend yourself.

SCENE CLOSES.

SCENE SECOND.

PARLOR IN FARMER JOHNSON'S HOUSE.

[ENTER 1ST R., JERUSHA JOHNSON AND ABBEY SMITH.]

Jerusha J.—Abbey Smith, you talk like a woman of the world.
I am astonished at a girl of your good sense; but as Mr. Goodman,
our dear preacher, says, "vanity of vanities, all is vanity."

Abbey S.—(*twisting her apron*). Well, it aint for a hired help like
me to be vanity, but I guess help kin feel sorry when their fellers
leave, just like others. I know Sam Roberts has allus been soft on
me, an' I've been soft on him; you'd be soft on him, too, Miss Gurusha, if you was me. Sam is the best felloh ——

Jerusha J.—There, there, Abbey Smith, not another word, you make me blush about your fellows. The day will come, when, as Mr. Goodman says, you will see "all is vanity." The world is fearfully wicked. Oh! how it has changed since I was young—I mean since I was a child. I am young still, Mr. Goodman says—

Abbey S.—Yes mum.

Jerusha J.—My nephew, John Johnson, has determined to fight. He is foolishly in love with Alice Gray, but as Mr. Goodman says, "'tis vanity." Now, John is going to war. John has drawn his sword, why can't Sam Roberts draw his sword.

Abbey S—I don't know, mum, but Sam has no sword except a hammer. Sam's a blacksmith.

Jerusha J.—Abbey, you provoke me. I speak in figures.

Abbey S.—Yes mum, that's the way Sam and me dance cortillons.

Jerusha J.—The Government will give him a sword. There are too many men in the world, let them kill each other off, except John and Mr. Goodman.

Abbey S.—Yes mum, there are too many men except Sam.

[ENTER LUCY JOHNSON, 1ST R.]

Lucy J.—Well, aunt, has Abbey been telling you that Sam Roberts is going to leave her?

Jerusha J.—Yes, my child, but as Mr. Goodman says, "all is vanity."

Lucy J.—I have been giving Solomon credit for that refreshing sentiment, aunt. But if you will pardon me, I should like to have the parlor to myself for a few moments. I am informed a visitor in the hall desires to see me alone for a moment.

[EXIT ABBEY S., 1ST L. JERUSHA J. CROSSING TO R.]

Jerusha J.—Some vile man. O that my niece would renounce the world, as Mr. Goodman says. [EXIT 1ST R.]

Alf. T.—[ENTER 1ST L.] Ah! Miss Lucy you are cruel to keep me waiting so long. But I am afraid by seeing you—

Lucy J.—Mr. Thornton will confer a favor by transacting his business with me as soon as possible. I have another engagement.

Alf. T.—I can imagine that engagement, Miss Lucy. I hope to sever it some day. I came to say that to-night I start south to be absent, Heaven only knows how long. I could not leave without coming to say farewell and to assure you of my love.

Lucy J.—Sir, I told you before this subject was offensive to me, why will you persist.

Alf. T.—Miss Lucy, let the depth of my devotion be my only excuse. I know I have been bad in many things, but pure in this, my worship of you. I go to fight in what I deem right, and ere I leave tell me you do not hate me, and that in hours of peril you will pray at least for my safety.

Lucy J.—I pray for your safety! I, whose brother and friends are going to fight against you, pray for your safety! Why Alfred Thornton, this is the very sublimity of impudence and cool effrontery. No, sir, while I shall invoke Heaven to bring peace to my country, I shall pray that justice be meted out to the bad men who have brought sorrow to my home and my heart. Leave me, Mr. Thornton, this subject is even more objectionable than that of your love.

Alf. T.—Miss Lucy, listen to me. I am not so bad that the slightest word you could utter would not make me a good man. I am a Southern man in feeling, but a *yes* from your lips would lead me to fight in any cause. The faintest hope of your love would make me respond to-morrow to Lincoln's call. If you would save me, Miss Johnson, Miss Lucy, do not cast me off without a hearing.

Lucy J.—Now, sir, I despise you. Your words confirm my worst fears of your utter want of principle. I can respect the Southern people who honestly act out their errors, but a man whose sword hangs on a woman's word when great principles are at stake, should not be trusted even by his friends.

Alf. T.—You are as cruel as you are beautiful. I have been a wanderer in the world without relatives or love till I met you. Is it not worth your while to try my salvation? Why crush me still lower, when you can raise me to your own level!

Lucy J.—I would save you, Mr. Thornton. I would do much to make you a good, true man. If you only change now I can give you the love of a sister.

Alf. T.—No more than a sister's love?

Lucy J.—No more than a sister's love is mine to give.

Alf. T.—Then the die is cast, and while blood flows through this right strong arm it will hold a sword against those you love, and while my heart beats its every throb will be hatred and death to Louis Ludlow. [EXIT 1ST L.]

Lucy J.—Yes, death to the man who saved your life. (*Solus.*) Oh! My Father above, that this fearful dream of death would pass away. One short month ago and who so happy as I! Home, brother and Louis! Now all seems dark as that time far away back when mother died. Oh, Louis, you must go, though it breaks my heart, my brave, noble Louis!

Abbey S.—[ENTER 1ST L.] Oh, Miss Lucy, you look so pale. I feel very pale too on account of Sam, though your aunt Gurusha says ''tis vanity.' Your vanity is at the door, Miss Lucy, Mr. Louis

Ludlow. He looks awful riled. Guess he met that other vanity, Thornton, down the road.

Lucy J.—Tell Mr. Ludlow to come in, Abbey.

[EXIT ABBEY S., 1st L.]   [ENTER LOUIS L., 1st L.]

Lucy J.—O, Louis! Welcome! Welcome! I have wanted you so much.

Louis L.—Lucy, why are you so excited? Has that man Thornton been here? Come, tell me all about it.

Lucy J.—O yes, Louis, he has been talking again. I know I ought not to have seen him. But I hoped I might be able to make him see the right.

Louis L.—You are the kindest girl in the world, and the best, but I am afraid, Lucy, you undertook too large a job in making Thornton a good man. He would have been in his grave to-day but for me ; yet, when I met him in the road as he left here, he passed me with a scowl and low mutterings of revenge.

Lucy J.—Promise me, Louis, you will not court a difficulty with him.

Louis L.—But if I meet him in arms against me, Lucy—

Lucy J.—Well, then, Louis, I would wound him in the arm so that he could not fight.

Louis L—(*laughing.*) Would it not be better to wound him so that he could not run.

Lucy J.—Well, as you say, Louis, but please don't kill any one. I do so hope no body will be killed in this fearful war.

Louis L.—(*laughing.*) It would certainly be a fearful war if there were no one killed. But, my darling, (*taking her hand*) if all the soldiers were like you, we would meet on the field, drop our arms and shake hands as we do and be friends, eh!

Lucy J.—Yes, indeed, Louis; but I want to tell you we have been making a beautiful flag. Alice Gray and myself bought the material. To-morrow, before you leave, we are going to present it to you. Wont you guard it for my sake?

Louis L.—For *your* sake! You selfish little mortal! I will guard it for the sake of the Union, and cherish that particular flag for my darling, and our own little Union—that is to be. But I must leave, we are enrolling men in the village and I must get back. Now good-by till to-morrow.

Lucy J.—Good-by, my own brave Louis. [EXIT.]

12

SCENE THIRD.

WOOD OR LANDSCAPE. MUSIC. ENTER TROOPS, 1ST L. STAGE MARCH OR DRILL. ENTER R. H. YOUNG LADIES WITH FLAG, VILLAGERS FOLLOWING.

Officer.—(*Commands,*) Attention! Color-guard, to the front, march.

[Color Bearer—Louis Ludlow ; Color Guards—Jackson Ludlow, Jack Johnson, Sam Roberts and Jim Hansom.]

Speech by Lucy J.—My friends, the flag which I hold in my hand is the emblem of our whole nation. Its glorious field of blue represents not only our own beloved Ohio, but every State in the North now arming for the defense, and every State in the South arrayed against us in Rebellion. This flag was wrought by your sisters' hands, is covered with our tears of sorrow at this parting, and hallowed by our prayers for its safety and your return. I need not tell you to guard it bravely, for I am convinced the brave men before me will protect its folds. You will return it in safety, and I pray God, that with it may come the brave color-guard to whom I intrust it. In the dark hours of battle look up to the God of justice. Look around on the land of our fathers and remember the sisters who bow for you in prayer.

Louis L.—Miss Johnson, permit me in behalf of my comrades, to thank you and the thoughtful ladies who co-operated with you in procuring this flag. We accept it with a full appreciation of the trust imposed through you by the nation. We are about to march for the scene of war, and we have that dread of death incident to all men who risk life for principle. One by one of the color-guard now standing before you may drop off by bullet or disease, but this glorious banner will fall to hands as brave. While God gives us strength to guard it, in the summer's march, the winter's bivouac and the battle's fearful storm, we will ever keep it pointed to that Heaven from which our greatest protection must come. With you, we pray that all may return in safety, bringing back the colors without a stain, and the news of a land preserved through our valor and firm devotion.

SONG. AIR—*Bruce's Address.*

Girls —Guard the flag, brothers brave,
From every traitor band,
With your swords dig the grave
For the foes of our land.
Think, in the battle's hour,
Of what our fingers wrought,

Flag of the Union's power,
  For which our forefathers fought.
Guard the flag! Guard the flag—
  Flag of the brave and free,
'Till it floats from every crag,
  From the lakes down to the sea.

Soldiers.—For this our swords we draw,
  For this our lives we'll give;
Till all wrong bows down to law.
  That liberty may live.
What if though this guard may die.
  What if thousands may be slain.
Still aloft this flag will fly
  Triumphant o'er the main.
We will guard the flag,
  Flag of the brave and free,
Till it floats o'er every crag
  From the lakes down to the sea.

CHORUS.

Girls. —Guard the flag! Guard the flag!
Soldiers.—We will guard this honored flag!
  Flag of the brave and free,
  Till it floats from every crag
  From the lakes down to the sea.

Color guard march back to position, while officer commands attention.
Carry arms. Present arms. BAND SALUTE. *Carry arms. Right face.*
Port arms. Break ranks. March.

Mr. L.—(*To Louis L.*)—Well, my boy, you have something to fight
for; may God bless you and bring you back in safety. But go,
Lucy is watching you. I must see Jackson and all the boys.

Louis L.—A short time, dear father, and I hope to return, bringing you the good news of a restored land. (*Joins Lucy J.*) Well,
Lucy, that was a beautiful speech of yours, and a beautiful flag
accompanied it.

Lucy J.—Certainly a beautiful flag, Louis, but do be careful for
my sake. Don't rush into danger unless there is a necessity, will
you? Please say you won't.

Louis L.—Rush into unnecessary danger. Why, you dear soul, I
have you to live for. Why should I expose myself. Now tell me
you will write very long gossipy letters, all about the village; and
you can tell me if Abbey Smith here gets another beaux instead of
Sam.

2

Abbey S.—No, thank you, Mr. Ludlow, I am satisfied with my vanity. Miss Gurusha is right, all the world is vanity to me. Isn't it, Sam?

Sam R—Your head is level there, Abbey. Here is something I want you to keep for my sake. (*Hands red handkerchief.*)

Abbey S.—I'll wear this night and day, even if Miss Gurusha does call it vanity.

(*Assembly is given.*)

Louis L.—The bugle sound; good-by my own own one.

Lucy J.—Good-by, Louis.

FAREWELL. *Soldiers shake hands with villagers. Battalion forms. Officer commands attention. Present arms. Carry arms. Batallion, right face.* MUSIC—"*Girl I left behind me.*" *Troops file off stage.* BUSINESS. *Villagers R. F. Soldiers in railroad car, with colors and guard on platform.*

TABLEAUX—THE RISING OF THE NORTH.

[CURTAIN.]

15

ACT II.

SCENE FIRST.

A Country Tavern in the Mountains of Tennessee. Alfred Thornton, Tom Flynn, Bob Mason, Long George, Peter Higgly and Mountain men discovered. (*Lively Music.*)

Alf. T.—No, friends, we have nothing to hope for from the Yankees of any party. Democrats and Republicans are equal in their hate and opposition.

Bob M.—See here, stranger, we uns har in the mountains aint much yer see on book larnin. But we kin read the trees and tell whin Spring's a leavin, or the winter a comin on. We uns kin look at the sky an' tell if thar's a goin' to be a storm, and we kin measure a man an' tell just how full he is of fight.

Alf. T.—I don't understand you, sir. You do not wish to insult me by saying I will not fight.

Bob M.—Sartin not, stranger. But we uns har in the mountains knows as how noise is harmless, and men as brags aint things to be skeered of.

Alf. T.--It was not my intention to scare any body, for I presume I am among friends.

Bob M.—Stranger, I've been presuming I'd be rich each yar since I were a boy, and dogened if I aint wantin' of money now as a hen is of horns. Why, you might as well try to build a pig pen out of cold mush as to do anythin' by presumin'.

Tom F.—Well, it's me sel' that's presumin' this blessed minit that this is the worst crowd I ever sit eyes on. Here we are, me sel' and Mr. Thornton, after thravellin' for tin days in the mountains of Kintucky ; lavin the Yankees behind us an' our comfortable homes, an' all to fight for yese. And now whin we gits into Tinnissee, shure yer not dacent enough to say Tom Flynn have yer mouth on ye. Now, before we have any more talking my sentiments are, let us have about three inches of unwatered hospitality, an' thin I'll show yes how the Flynns kin talk wud their machinery in ordLer.

Long G.—Yes, stranger, lets all licker up. We'uns forgot that ye'r might want suthin. Heah, I'll stan treat this time.

[Business.]

Mountaineer.—Now, stranger, jest let we'uns har that story of yourn, an all about them dam'd Yankees.

Alf T.—I lived for some time past peacefully on the Ohio river, within sight of the Sunny South. I would have remained there all my life, had not the South been wronged; had not you men been deprived of your rights; had not your liberties been assailed and your homes threatened. Friends when I think of the outrage I was subjected to in leaving the North to join you, it quite unmans me.

Tom F.—Mr. Thornton, Mr. Thornton, shure ye put too little whiskey in that last glass of water ye tuk. Now before lettin yer feelings get the bether of ye, my advice is to return this gintleman's threat, and thin yes kin go on would a clear conscience, knowin' yer not in debt.

Alf T.—Ah, Tom, you are always right. Come up, friends, drink with me.

[Liquor is poured out. Tom F drinks his and takes Pete H.'s. Peter picks up glass and tries to drink. Looks into his tumbler and all around it, then asks for bottle, pours out more whisky, while handing bottle back Tom F. subs itutes a glass of water for the whisky. Peter raises his g ass, tastes it, looks in and around it.]

Peter H.—Mein Gott in Himmel vas is das. I puds viskey in mein glass one dime, und ven I trinks dere is de glass, but dunner, der is no viskey; und ven I puds some more viskey mit mein glass, der is vasser, aber der is no viskey. Ich kon nicht vy dis is so, aber es ist war.

Alf T.—Yes, my friends, if you will listen to me, your hate for the cowardly Yankees will become more intense, and your determination stronger to resist them. The day the news came to our village that the South dared to assert her rights by firing on the Stars and Stripes, the emblem of abolition and oppression, I dared, as a freeman, to express my feelings for the South. But was I permitted to go on? No! a hundred cowards, with a rope to hang me, gathered around and threatened my life. I had but one friend, brave Tom Flynn, the man who accompanied me here.

Tom F.—Yer right there, Mr. Thornton. It was yersel had always a dollar an' a dhrink for Tom. An' talking about dhrinks, Mr. Thornton, sorrow one of me is dhry at all at all, but for the sake of the illegant gintlemen around me I could dhrink the lakes of Killarnee dhry. Providen, of course, that the lakes were made of potheen instead of nasty wather.

Bob M.—Strangers, I'll liquor this time. I aint much for whisky. I'd as soon eat a young un with the whoopin' cough as drink alone. But I'll stan' this for all hands an' to dry up that are feller who will gab like an ole woman with the toothache. Come up all on you an' drink, p'raps for the last time with Bob Mason.

Alf. T.—Glad of the honor Mr. Mason.

Long G.—Bob aint heavy on the drink, but, sar, start him on anything else an' ye'd better git out of his way.

[Liquor is poured out. Bob Mason lays his glass down, when Tom F. after drinking his own takes Mason's, without apparently looking Mason reaches out his left hand and grasps Tom's arm with such force that the glass falls to the floor. Tom F. gives a howl of pain.]

Bob M.—See here, you dogoned little cuss. Yeh kin play tricks on men as walks with their eyes closed, an' lies down with their eyes open. I don't kar for the whiskey any mor'n an eagle does for lightnen. But if I bought a case of small pox for my own use I'd have it in my own family spite of all the docters and thieves in the mountain. Now git.

Tom F.—Oh, by gar. yeh have the dumdest grip I ever saw at all at all. Sure, avick, I did'nt mane to take yer whiskey. It is not in our family to wrong any man out of a dhrink. Here's my hand on it.

Peter H.—Ich weis nicht. aber Ich tinks I knows wer hat mein viskey und der tam scamp has verkauft mich mit das vasser.

Mountaineer.—The stranger will never git through with his story, if you uns keep a 'sturbin' him this way. Pile in with your story stranger.

Alf. T.—When the Yankees threatened to hang me I pulled out these, (*displaying pistols*) and facing them, dared them all and the cowards fell back. I told them then I intended going into Tennessee to raise a company of mountain men to battle for the South. For long days and nights I have traveled to reach here. I am now among you. Who is willing to join me?

[*All except Bob M and Long George shout* I, I, I, stranger.]

Mountaineer.—Bob Mason, aint you and Long George agoing to join us to fight for Tennessee?

Bob M.—I aint a man of book larnin' like this stranger, whose tongue is as smooth as ice, an' as dangerous, while his heart is as hard and as cold, but afore I fight the Yankees, I want to know whar they have wronged me and mine. My young 'uns are safe on the mountain, au' I kin come an' go, with none to stop me. Long ago I heerd my father speak of Gineral Jackson and the whole Union, an' by that I'm goin' to stan'. I have no slaves, nor would 'nt have if I could. I allus thought it sneakin' to steal the game killed by another man's rifle. This is a rich man's quarrel, let the rich men fight for the South. I'll stan' by the Union, an' it'll be some unhealthy for the cuss that tries to stop me.

2*

18

Mountaineer.—If yer wus North, Bob Mason, they'd hang you.

Alf T.—Yes, and if the brave men South did their duty they would hang him where he stands.

[*Crowd.*—Shoot the scoundrel. Hang him up. Cut his heart out. They rush at him with knives and pistols. Bob Mason with Long George beside him, coolly backs against the wall, a pistol in each hand.] [EXIT TOM F. AND PETER H. HURRIEDLY.]

Bob M.—You cowards and skunks, to turn on a mountain man for darin' to do right. Back there, or by the ghost of Gineral Jackson, I'll send daylight through you. (*To Thornton*). Out of my path; Long George and me is goin' North whar you cum'd from, and let the devil tempt none of you to stop me. Keep along side, George. The cowards know me too well to shoot. We 'uns will return an' look out, you cowards, when we light the signal for the hunt on the mountain.

SCENE SECOND.

ROAD OR LANDSCAPE. [ENTER 1ST L.]

Peter H.—Dat Irishman trinks visky alle sames Ich trinks lager. It vas so strange, I pig oop mine glass, dere is notting, und ven I pigs it opp vonce more, der is vasser, und I shoost tinks Peter vas der teufel in de madder mid de trinks.

[ENTER TOM FLYNN, 1ST L., SINGING.]

AIR—*Hill of Glen O'Kery.*

Och, my name is bould Morgan McCarty, from Thrim,
Me relations all died except one brother, Jim,
An' he's gone a fightin' away to Cabul,
Faith I fear he's laid low wid a nick in his skull.
But let him be dead or be liven,
Some prayers for his soul I'll be given,
That'll sind him sthraight over to heaven,
　　For he left me this darlin' ould sthick.

Och, if this sthick had a tongue,
Shure it could tell ye some tales,
How it schmothered the countenances of the O'Nales;
It made bits of skull to fly up in the air,
It was the promother of fun at aich fair;
For I swear by the toe nails of Moses
It often broke bridges of noses—
Of the factions that dared to oppose us,
　　Mysel' an' my darlin' ould sthick.

Och, the last time I ued it wuz on Patrick's day,
Larry Fagan and I we got on a sphray,
We went to a fair 'tother side of Atbray,
An' we danced, an' wnin dun, I kissed Kate McAray.
An' her thrue love ran out for his cousin:
By the 'tarnel he brought in a dozen,
An' they'd knocked us into a doldhreen,
　　Hadn't it been for my darlin' ould sthick.

Tom F. (discovering Peter II.)—Ye'r there, are ye? Well, I'll say it, an' whin a Flynn says it, ye may bet it's thrue. ivery word. I've thraveled across the ocean, an' I've seen heavy dhrinkin' at home, but for a pussy little Dutchman, ye can jist wear the color. Och. by the pipers, it's yersel' kin change the location of whiskey without so much as winkin'. an' ye'r not dhrunk! Well, by my conscience, I respect yer capacity, as Jonah said to the whale.

Peter II. (angrily).—Ich weirs nicht was sie sagen, du swein. Was for you trinks mein viskey, and was for you puds vaaser in mein glass, you bese von tam tief.

Tom F.—Now kape your breath to cool your stir about, an' do'nt, if ye value yer life, provoke Tom Flynn to fight. Shure if I wuz to lay me paw on ye, divil a one of ye'd have time to offer up a prayer till ye'd be where dhrinks are scarcer an' more needed than in Aist Teunessee. (*In a milder tone.*) But, come here, let us be friens, an' tell me if yer parients are livin'; an' how many childhren ye have the dead image of yersel'. And avick, jist inform me if ye could lone a decent mimber of my family a dollar and fifty cents for one hour an' a half. I'm expecting money, (*aside*) musha, God knows it's mesel' has been expecting it for many a day.

Peter II.—(*Reaching out his hand*) I dout vant to make a fuss mit you. You're all richt. But I gets gross mid so much drubbie all de dime.

Tom F.—Come over and lane on me, an if ye have any trubble jist pour it out to me as ye would to yer own blessed mother.

Peter II.—Vel I tinks some dings all de dime. Ven I comes mit dis land I choins de Mericans un I takes vat you call de oat.

Tom F.—Will, yer not a native American thin. Well upon my conscience ye talk so well I thought ye a lively Aist Tennessee Mountaineer.

Peter II.—No, Ich komt from Deutchland aber Ich bin ein Americaner by dis paber. Read de paber.

(*Hands Tom a paper. Tom pretends to read and turns it about in his*) *hands.*

Tom F.—Well, whats this shure Me eyes aint as young as they used to be.

Peter H.—Vy das ist mein allegiance, de paber mit vich I makes mine vote at de polls in lectin time.

Tom F.—You take that paper to the polls?

Peter H.—O, yah, all de dime.

Tom F.—Well, I in sorry yer a foreigner and dont understan the Inglish tongue. Ive been voten since the day I landed, and dom'd if I iver had to take an oath, or git a dirty bit of paper like that to do it.

Peter H.—But vot shall I do, shall I go mit de Union, or mit de State, I have very much drubble bout dat.

·*Tom F.*—Arrah, me frien, give yersel no thrubble about goin with the Union or the Sthate, but give me the dollar and fifty ciuts ye promised, an go wid me an I'll dbrink yer health iu a bumper.

(*Exit 2nd R. Peter opening his Pocket Book.*)

SCENE THIRD.

ROCKY PASS WITH SET ROCKS AND FIRE. BOB MASON, LONG GEORGE, FATHER ALLEN AND REFUGEES DISCOVERED.

Long G.—Wall, I'm right smart glad we're in Kaintuck. Hope that Thornton and his houn's won't chase us any more. Kaintuck's neutral. Ain't for fighten nobody.

Bob M.—Ye can't make a mountain cat look like a deer, nor squeeze fire so that as to take it for water. Kaintuck is crouching on the hill top like a lynx, and which ever side she springs on look out. Though it may be that there is a lynx wanten' to go at each side. Then I say look out for a fight between the lynxs.

Father A.—Already we have lost many of our number to reach this place, but we can only be safe under the flag I carried as a soldier in the everglades of Florida.

Bob M.—Don't be cast down father Allen. We'uns will stan' by you like as lookout by the Tennessee. The men are posted on guard, and if we are attacked again to-night, God pity the men that drive us to bay.

Father A.—I know you are brave, Bob, but what are we against so many. Our friends are slain on the mountains, or hanging to the pines on the hill sides. I do not like this place; there is no chonce for retreat.

Bob M.—No, father, no chance for retreat; thar is no need for retreat. Night an' day they have driven us from our homes and families, and my heart is sore with our sufferings and wrongs. Better die like brave men heah in Kaintuck, than be dogged still farther through the mountains, with sore feet an' starvin' inwards, an' hearts full of sorrow. Better die whar the ring of our rifles will echo near our own mountains, than fall off one by one, a prey to the blood hounds who chase us.

Long G.—That talk suits me, Bob. I'm out of Tennessee, and doggoned if I want to run any more.

Fugitives.—It suits me. And me. And me.

Father A.—God bless you my brave boys. Come about the fire. (*Listening.*) Hark, I heard a yell away down the mountain. Did you hear it, Bob?

Bob. T.—No, father Allen, it was the wind I reckon blown around the rocks. I often hear it so in the mountains a night.

Father A.—Well, I am getting kind of old, I reckon, and I aint young, an' I feel the walken' an' starven' more than younger men. Though I will say, Bob, I have eaten more of your bread than you have yoursel'. (*Listens.*) I did hear a sound Bob, I am not mistaken. It comes from towards Cumberland Gap.

(*Bob Mason stepping out, shouts to a vidette alone on the rocks.*)

Bob M.—Tom Dawson, Tom Dawson.

Echo.—Hello!

Bob M.—Can you see down the valley?

Echo.—I can sir.

Bob M.—What do you see?

Echo.—A light on the mountain.

Bob M.—All right, shout if it comes near.

Echo.—I will.

Father A.—I want to speak to all, for I feel the hour of our parting will soon come.

(*Fugitives gather about Father Allen.*)

Long G.—Speak out father Allen, we are listening.

Father A.—You know that it will be death to fall into Thornton's hands.

Fugitives.—We do.

Father A.—You know it will be death to return to Tennessee without the flag.

Fugitives.—We do. We do.

Father A.—Let us bind ourselves together by an oath before Heaven, as we are now bound by our feelings. Are you willing to swear to stand by the last man till death, and the Union through life.

Fugitives.—We are. We are.

Father A.—Bob give me the old flag.

(*Bob Mason takes flag from hunting pouch and hands father Allen.*)

Father A.—All lay your hands on this flag and repeat after me.

(*All lay their hands on the flag and uncover their heads, as Father Allen speakes in a slow solemn voice, with his face raised.*)

Father. A—In the presence of God, here in his mountain temples, I pledge my wordly goods, and stand ready to lay down my life, to defend this flag, which I swear to protect as the emblem of the whole Union. And I promise before Heaven always to stand by my brothers who are here, and to permit neither myself nor them to be captured alive by the Rebels. And if God spares my life, day and night, winter and summer, in sunshine and in rain, I will battle with this one heart object: to bring the flag in triumph to Tennessee, and every part of the Union. Asking God to bless and guard us, we swear.

(*Bob Mason ties the flag to a stick and fastens it in the rocks, while doing so a shot is heard from the mountains.*)

Echo.—They are coming. All about us.
Bob M.—Come down, come. (*To Long George.*) Call in the guards. Here father Allen stand near this rock where you will be safe. I think the day is breaking.

(*Shooting heard in the distance. Guards rush in.*)

1st Guard.—Thornton is close by. Oh, God, we are lost.

[Bob Mason cooly raises his rifle and fires. The rest follow and fire briskly. A cry of pain is heard as fugitives fall back, and Father Allen falls dying, with face to the mountain.]

Tableaux—TROOPS MARCHING UP THE MOUNTAIN.

Father A.—Now, oh, Lord, I can die in peace, the flag has come back to Tennessee.

Slow Music.—CURTAIN.

ACT III.

SCENE FIRST.

Slow Music.

PARLOR IN FARMER JOHNSON'S HOUSE. JERUSHA JOHNSON, LUCY JOHNSON, ALICE GRAY, SUSAN MARIA HANSOM, AND OTHER LADIES, DISCOVERED SEWING AND KNITTING.

Jerusha J.—I am not suprised at anything now. Two years ago when the war broke out, if any one had told me Mr. Goodman would have dressed up in fancy clothes and gone off for a Chaplain, I would have said he is a man of peace, and looks on all those things as vanity. So, Lucy, I am not surprised that you want to leave and go down into those wild mountains to nurse men. Oh, when I was young—I mean when I was a child, young girls were not so reckless as they are now.

Lucy J.—Aunt, I am sorry you should consider me reckless. The lines of duty and desire do not always run parallel. I would prefer for my own comfort to remain in this quiet home, working with you and my friends to show the soldier boys we do not forget them. But, when I read of terrible battles and the suffering wounded, suffering for me and you, Aunt, I feel duty calling me from comfort to hardship, that I may minister to other brothers and friends, as I would have mine cared for.

Jerusha J.—Well, well, I suppose I would do the same thing. I wonder if Chaplains have to fight.

Alice G.—I hope they do. I know I would not want to wear the uniform if I could not fight.

Lucy J.—Why, you dear child, you have no thought of donning the uniform, have you?

Alice G.—No, not exactly. But if Mother were well I would not remain here a day. I feel sometimes when I read of terrible marches and cold nights on picket, that I would like to rest a soldier by carrying his knapsack, or acting for him on guard. (*Turning to Lucy.*) By-the-way, Lucy, dear, have you fully made up your mind to go?

Lucy J.—Yes, and I have decided to start for Chattanooga to-morrow.

Susan Maria.—Well, now, Lucy, ye'll see my Jim Hansom down there, and I want you to tell him to be awful keerful and not run into danger. Whin he writ last time he tole me he kem nigh bein' shot in the hat. Just think how close that is to Jim's head. You know, Lucy, he always would wear his hat over his eyes. Try an' get Jim not to do so any more.

Alice G.—Better have a ball near his hat, Susan Maria, than a brick in it.

Susan Maria.—I do say, Alice Gray, you'r the queerest gal I ever seed. What would my Jim be doing with a brick in his hat.

Alice G.—Why, Susan Maria, the bricks are supposed to be mixed with whiskey, and are carried for the heat and the cold. And men put them in their hats when they feel sleepy, and too wide awake, and when they feel happy, and tired, and—

Susan Maria..—Why, sakes alive, Alice Gray, I do hope my Jim will have one of them bricks in his hat all the time, (*laughter*)

(*Enter Abbey Smith 1st R.*)

Abbey S.—Oh, Miss Lucy, Mr. Ludlow an' Mr. Williams, an' Mr. Johnson, your dear father, an' Mr. Gray, an' they all says are you ready to see them, an' Miss Lucy when are you going away, an' will you be sure to see my vanity. I have something for him.

Lucy J.—Your vanity, why what do you mean you silly girl.

Abbey S.—(*Covering face with apron.*) Oh, you know Miss Lucy.

Lucy J.—How should I know, you foolish thing?

Abbey S.—Sam Roberts, he's my vanity. Oh, if Sam was to git hurt, I declare to goodness I'd take laudlum, or go down there an' just tear the eyes out of them nasty rebels.

Jerusha J.—There, there, Abbey Smith, you make me blush. What is this world coming to. Tell the gentlemen to walk in.

Abbey S.—Yes mum. [EXIT 1ST R.]

[ENTER 1ST R. SQUIRE WILLIAMS, FARMER JOHNSON, MR. LUDLOW AND MR. GRAY. *They shake hands with the Ladies.* ENTER 1ST R. ABBEY SMITH.]

Squire W.—Hard at work. Now, thats right. I believe in doing everything to restore the Union. Susan Maria you know that. Didn't I send Jim Hansom off at once? Yes, and I'd send every relative in the world.

Mr. L.—No body can doubt your patriotism Squire. They say Morgan is coming this way from Indiana. Of course you will turn out to fight him.

(*Jerusha Johnson screams, and Abbey Smith gives her a drink.*)

Squire W.—Jim Hansom ought to be here. When I was young,

Mr. Ludlow, I could fight. I dar'd an Englishman one time to come into my yard. But now, now, Mr. Ludlow, I'm too old. And then the school. You see I'm a trustee.

Farmer J.—That's true, Squire, the country could'nt get along without you. And a good school director is hard to get; but I have one boy a fighter for the Union, an' here's my girl Lucy again to leave me like a little angel to keer for the wounded. I aint no better than my children, and if John Morgan comes this way I'll help to make it tough work carryin' war into Ohio. Darn me if I don't. (*Quickly.*) Excuse me, ladies, but of late I often feel like cussen.

Jerusha J.—Oh, brother, what will become of the country if you are so wicked.

Alice G.—I just wish I was a man sometimes, Mr. Johnson.

Farmer J.—Why, Alice, what would Jack do if you were. What do you want to be a man for?

Alice G.—Why I would like to sit down and swear at the Rebels till I calmed myself.

Jerusha J.—Oh, when I was young; I mean when I was a girl; young folks did'nt dare to talk so. What is this world coming to.

Mr. L.—By-the-way, Lucy, I heard from Louis to-day. He desired me to say he wrote you at the same time. He goes into raptures over that noble fellow, Bob Mason, whom they rescued in the mountain two years ago. I often think of that occurrence, and I hope before the war closes the death of that old man they called father Allen, may be avenged.

Lucy J.—Yes, I heard from Louis this morning. He informs me that a great fight is daily expected. I am the more anxious to get off, so as to be there in time.

Jerusha J.—Come, girls, bundle up your work, next week we meet at Mr. Gray's.

Mr. G.—Where I shall be happy to have you.

Alice G.—Oh, before putting away these socks I wish to put this letter in. It will do some brave boy good to read it. Lucy, darling, I will not bid you good by. To-morrow I will be over to see you.

Squire W.—Yes, we will all be over to see her off. She has the sort of pluck I like. [EXIT ALL BUT SQUIRE W., *Jerusha J.* and *Abbey S.*] Oh, if I was only young. (EXIT.)

Jerusha J.—O, if I was only young. But all is vanity. (EXIT.)

Abbey S.—Oh, if I was only Mrs. Robert's vanity. (EXIT.)

3

SCENE SECOND.

LANDSCAPE OR WOOD.

Bob M.—(ENTER 1ST L.) By the ghost of Gineral Jackson, this looks bad for me. Was an August frost, or a broken water wheel an' no flour in the mill. Who'd have thought of Rebels so near our lines. I had to run like a stag before the blood houn's last night, an' now, when I thought mysel all safe, the dogon'd grey cusses are all around me like the measels. If I kin jest get into our lines, we'uns will be ready; if I don't, may the Lor' help us, for the're a comin' down powerful strong, like a mountain river arter a July rain. Hist, there. (*Lays hand on pistol,*) I'll try this way, (*turns to right.*) Thar I see 'em gropen along an' moven roun' this way by the hill. If I had my rifle I'd make it onpleasant for a few of 'em afore they gits up. (*Goes Left. Shot heard. Bob Mason springs back, drawing pistol. Shout is heard.*) Yell away, yeh dogon'd sneaks. Ye'll find I'm harder to git than a catfish on the mountain top.

[Shot heard. Bob Mason springs back and fires. Enter Rebel squad 1st L. Bob Mason fires, killing officer in command. Retreats Right, when more Rebels enter 1st R, and surround him.

Lieut. of Rebels.—Surrender, surrender, you Yankee bush whacker.

Bob M.—(*Unfastening his belt and laying down his pistols*) Thar, that's all yeh kin have at present, as the catamount said whin they took his skin off.

Lieut. of R.—We will not only have your skin, but your life. (*Turning to his men.*) This is Bob Mason, the scout. Bring a rope here, boys, we will soon make short work of him. Blast him, that firing was too close to the Yankee lines. Keep a good watch down there.

Echo.—All right, sir.

[Rebels take off Bob Mason's coat and hat, then bind his hands behind his back and fasten rope about his neck.]

Lieut. of R.—You have killed Thomas Ludlow, one of my bravest men. You have been a curse to this region. Have you anything to say before you die?

Bob M.—I aint much at speakin', wimen, that live a long time, an' cowards have heaps of gab. I've done nothin' to bring a blush to my cheek since I was born. I have fought for the Union, an' my only sorrow at dyin' is that I can't live to help her more. I once had a hut in the mountain, an' a wife an' children. I loved my little home an' my wife an' babies, but you uns hunted me down like a stag, from hill to hill, till I left the State. An' then like cowards, in the cold winter, you uns'burned my hut to the groun', an' my wife an' little ones starved in the mountain. My heart has long carried a fire lit by the men who ruined me an' mine. I've paid you. I'm willin' to be at rest, an' meet them up thar.

Lieut. of Rebels.—Swing him up men. (*Men prepare to execute Bob Mason, when a cheer is heard.*) Quick, men, the Yankees are coming.

[Shots heard, the man fastening the rope falls wounded. Rebels rally for an instant, then fall back, when Louis Ludlow dashes on with Union soldiers.]

Louis L.—(*Frees Bob Mason.*) Hello Bob. We came just in time.

Bob M.—I was never so glad to see frien's in my life, as the bar said to the honey bees.

Louis L.—I had command of our advance picket post. I heard the firing some time ago, and reported to the officer in command. He sent me out to ascertain what it was. I hurried on and as I came up the hill I saw that wounded fellow with the rope about to hang you.

Bob M.—(*looking at wounded Rebel.*) He knows somebody saw him right smart at that time. There's another fellow dead over thar.

Louis L.—(*Crossing and examines dead Rebel.*) Merciful Heaven, Bob, you have killed my brother. This is Tom my poor brave misguided Tom. (*Kneels besides the body and feels his heart.*) Dead, dead, dead. Oh, Tom, God knows how I would have saved you at the risk of my life. Your heart my brother was always right. (*Rising.*) There is no time for sorrow, here boys we must carry the body back, bring a couple of muskets. (*Bis.*)

Bob M.—Sergeant afore Heaven I did nt know he was your brother. My hand would wither afore it would be raised 'gainst you or yours.

Louis L.—(*Seizing Bob Mason's hand.*) You did your duty Bob, may every soldier do his as well. But that poor boy was my brother, and bitterly as I hate this rebellion, I could not raise my rifle against him. My poor father when you hear of this.

(ALL EXIT CARRYING BODY AND GUARDING PRISONER WHO LIMPS.)

28

SCENE THIRD.

MUSIC.—*Yankee Doodle.* DARK WOOD.

[A Union skirmish line advances across the the stage firing. A regiment appears, with Louis Ludlow carrying the colors, deploys in line of battle and advances. Before crossing stage Union skirmishers are driven back. The regiment halts and fires a volley on the Rebels who advance with a yell. The regiment falls back, Louis Ludlow and several Union soldiers drop. Louis Ludlow drops colors also. *Music.—Dixie.* The Rebels charge on stage and after Union troops who retreat off to right, Rebels following. Noise of battle gradually dies off in distance.]

Louis L.—(*Rising in wonder and feeling bleeding head.*) Where am I, where is the regiment. (*Hears Rebel yells.*) Oh God we are beaten. The colors where are the colors. (*Looks around and picks them up.*) The enemy is falling back this way; my flag. The flag I swore a traitors hand should never touch, must it be disgraced now? No, no. Now God give me strength. (*Takes flag from the staff and opens his breast.*) Here near my heart I will wear it. Here till I die I will carry the colors. (*Conceals flag in breast.*) They must not see the staff. Ah, there's a hollow log. *Hides flag staff, then falls pressing his hand to his head.*)

[ENTER REBEL OFFICER WITH SQUAD.]

Lieut. of R.—(*looking over the line.*) The enemy is advancing in force, see they are pushing back our centre. (*Cheer is heard.*) They have captured Nolen's Battery. I fear the day is lost. Take this prisoner to the rear quick. [EXIT LEFT WITH LOUIS LUDLOW.]

MUSIC.—*Star Spangled Banner.*

[Rebel troops fall back firing to the left of stage, Union troops charge.] TABLEAUX.

ACT IV.

SCENE FIRST.

Plain Chamber. Richmond, Va. Plaintive Music. Lucy Johnson and Capt. Alfred Thornton discovered.

Alf. T.—Well, Miss Johnson, I hope the men have treated you well since your capture near Knoxville. I had charge of you, and but for me you would have been hanged as a spy after you were captured roaming among the wounded. Do you know where you are now?

Lucy J.—I do not, sir.

Alf. T.—You are in the city of Richmond, Virginia. You have made the tour from Tennessee with Longstreet's corps. We had to fall back before the Yankees, under that scoundrel Burnside, but we got nearly even with him. I suppose you know we captured Louis Ludlow near Knoxville. He was in our hands for some time. I tried to save him but he died a few days since of his wound.

Lucy J.—(*Pressing her hand to her forehead.*) Go on sir, tell me why you have intruded.

Alf T.—From no desire to annoy you, Miss Johnson. Every care bestowed upon you up to this time has been through my influence. I have saved you from insult and disgrace, and I have watched over you when you dreamt no friend was nigh. Even now there are charges against you as a spy. They can be proved; but your life and honor must depend on the reply you give me.

Lucy J.—Mr. Thornton I left my home on a holy mission to care for the wounded, who might fall for my country. I learned that Louis Ludlow was dying on the field before Knoxville and went to his aid. Your men took me prisoner and carried me here. You are the moving spirit in this matter, and my death will be on your head.

Alf T.—Louis Ludlow I respected as a brave man. He is dead, and his fate lies before you if you do not accept me as a friend. (*Draws near and tries to take her hand.*) Oh, Lucy, I have loved you with an intensity weaker natures could not feel. Day and night since I left you, your image has haunted me, and to win even a smile from you I would sacrifice all else that's worldly.

Lucy J.—Sir, I desire no more of this; it is cowardly thus to in-

3*

sult me with the memory of the dead in my heart. I desire to be tried, believing that the Southern men are brave and honorable, believing that only your falsehood and wicked designs have kept me a prisoner. Leave me, sir, at once. Your very presence is worse than death.

Alf T.—Not so fast, Miss Johnson, not so fast. For three weeks, though you knew it not, I have been your escort, and my comrades laughed and winked when I approached in the evening's camp the wagon that contained you. Even if you should be dismissed after trial you will leave with a stain and a dishonor on your name.

Lucy J.—Oh you are brave thus to insult a helpless girl (*holding up her arms.*) My arms are weaker than yours, and there is no one stronger here to protect me. But here, here in my heart I am conscious of my honor and purity. And up there at the judgment seat I can stand feeling that I have tried to do my duty, knowing that by word or deed I have never wronged the humblest of God's creatures. Now Mr. Thornton are you prepared to do the same?

Alf. T.—You will drive me mad if you talk so. If I sink the lowest of men it is you who have driven me to it. If I rise regretting the errors I ask God to forgive it must be through you. You, with no tie that can bind you to the dead, can save me. (*Goes to the door and sees that it is secure.*) Lucy I have ever regretted drawing my sword against the cause you love. Give me hope. Tell me that you may regard me, and to-night I will make arrangements whereby we may escape to the Federal lines. Once there I will fight for the Union nerved by the hope of your love, and you can watch me from the protection of your honor.

Lucy J.—Sir, I respect a brave man, fighting honestly in any cause. I despise a villain, though he stands in the pulpit. No cause would make you good. No sword would make you brave. You are as devoid of patriotism as you are of honor. If there be one spark of the love left you bore your mother, leave me. Leave me.

Alf. T.—(*Excitedly.*) Yes, I will leave you, you decide your own fate. Death awaits you, or worse, a disgrace which will cling to your name and follow you to your grave, and my curse, the curse of a life you have blasted, will follow you forever. Death has no longer a dread for me, and it will be sweet if it comes with the anguish of those you love. Louis Ludlow is not dead. (*Lucy starts, and clasping her hands, looks up, as if in prayer.*) He is here, within hearing distance of your voice, a prisoner in the Libby. Down below its gloomy rooms there are damp cells, where no ray of light ever enters. I know Turner, and through him I will place Ludlow where the green slime will cover him, and where, a yellow manacled skeleton, he will pray for death. Think this over, his fate is in your hands. To-morrow I will call again. [EXIT 1ST R.]

Lucy J.—(*Solus.*) Oh, if I could die! It seems as if my poor heart would break! Louis! my own brave Louis! God knows I would die to save you! Oh, Father of all, guard him, protect me. (*Starting.*) A noise! Who comes there?

[ENTER 1ST R. TONEY, *who closes the door carefully, while Lucy retreats with an expression of fear.*]

Toney—(*bowing.*) Don't be skeered of me, Miss. I aint white like Cap'n Thornton.

Lucy J.—Who are you? What do you want here?

Toney.—I am Toney, Cap'n Thornton's colored boy. I heard him, Miss. I was at de door when he talked so. 'Fore Heaben, Cap'n Thornton's a bad man. It won't be safe for you to stay heah, no how. Miss, I'se only a poor colo'd boy, an' I don't know much, but I does know dat up dar dere's a God, who'll judge me bi'ne bye, an' I does know dat my heart is good. Eber since Lincum's 'clamation, I'se wanted to clar out and go whar dar's liberty fur all men ob ebery colo'. I knows how good, like an angel, yeh's bin a keerin' fur de wounded. I hab slept ebery night like a watch dog, under de wagon yeh wuz in, an' I said to God I'd die afore any wrong came to yeh.

Lucy J.—I have seen you before.

Toney.—Yes, Miss. Now let me say dar's heaps ob danger heah wid dat bad man. You kin 'scape to de Yankee lines.

Lucy J.—Escape! How?

Toney.—I knows all de country down to Fort Monroe; been ober it many a time. Afore two days from to-night yeh kin be in de Yankee lines, if yeh is willin' to b'lieve. Toney will be a friend. (*Draws a small pistol from his pocket. Lucy starts back frightened.*) Heah, Miss, am a pistol, all loaded. See! If yeh say yeh'll 'scape keep dat ar' an' sen' a bullet to Toney's heart if he aint true as de sun. I swear afore Heaben to be yer slave till I takes yeh out ob danger.

Lucy J.—I believe you are good. But tell me! How can we get off?

Toney.—I'll git a mule to-night and put you on, about twelve o'clock, and tote yeh out whar no one will see, an' den, outside de lines I'll walk and jes make dat ar mule git. I knows all de culled people. Dey'le help me.

Lucy J.—I will trust you. To-night at twelve o'clock. (*She takes pistol and conceals it.*)

Toney.—Yes, Miss, I'll be at de winder

[EXIT 1ST R.]

Lucy J.—Oh, Louis, if you were only with me now.

[EXIT 1ST L.]

SCENE SECOND.

[Room in Libby Prison. Louis Ludlow discovered talking to a Fellow Prisoner. Other Prisoners in the back ground.]

Louis L.—We kept it secret up to this time. To-night we are going out.

Prisoner.—You astound me, Lieutenant. Please explain it.

Louis L.—To begin with, I am not a Lieutenant. I gave my name as as officer, hoping to escape with the colors I still carry, and believing I can make it right after I get out. Now this tunnel we have been working on for over a month, Col. Rose of the Seventy-seventh Pennsylvania planned. By removing the bricks in the wall of the floor below this we descended into the basement. Once there we cut through the foundation and made the street. We came up the east, near that warehouse where the boxes are stored. I have worked there nearly every night, now, thank God, it is completed. You must be ready to go out to-night.

Prisoner.—Thank you, Ludlow, I will be ready. May I tell a friend of mine?

Louis L.—O yes, but if too many know it, I am afraid none of us can get out. By the way, here is a friend. I must leave you.

[Enter Bob Mason, 2d L., disguised as a negro, with a pail and broom. Another black man, carrying a pan, from which smoke arises. Bob Mason and Louis Ludlow walk aside. Prisoners conversing in back ground.]

Louis L.—Bob, you have kept me nervous every day since you came here, and now, on the eve of my escape, I think more of your safety than I do of my own.

Bob M.—It is easy to have a stout heart whin thar's no danger. Mine grows stronger whin I think of saven you, an' your's will not flutter whin you git out under the stars and feel God's fresh air a blowen on your cheek, an' know you are free. I'd die if I wuz a pris'ner as many brave men is dyin' here.

Louis L.—You know where the tunnel comes up near the warehouse!

Bob M.—I reckon I does. I've been a watchin' to see dirt raised thar for a week.

Louis L.—To-night stand near the canal, dressed as a rebel soldier. Have a grey coat ready for me, and when the guard calls, " Half past one—Post number ten—All's well, ' watch, I will be coming out of the tunnel.

Bob M.—I'll watch, an' I'll have suthin' more'n a coat. I've 'ranged to git some pistols and cartridges, besides plenty of fodder. Don't take none of this dogon'd iron clad corn bread you'ns have to eat beah. It's powerful ruinin' on the teeth.

Louis L.—Be careful Bob. Your detection would be certain death.

Bob. M.—I'll be keerful on your account. I used to fear death, but thar's not much to make it skeery now. I saw Thornton yesterday, the sneaken cuss. He didn't know me, but I jis wanted to look him in the eye an' tell him what I thought on him.

Louis L.—Time will make all things even. Wait.

Bob. M.—(*Sweeping floor.*) I will, till—Half past one. Post No. Ten. All's well.

[ENTER 2D L., REBEL GUARD. EXIT 2D L., BOB MASON AND NEGRO.]

Officer Prison Guard.—Turn out for roll call, you Yankees. (*To prisoner on floor.*) Here, get up, you dog, and go to roll call.

Prisoner.—I am sick, I cannot move. Let me off this time.

Officer Prison Guard.—Here, guards, use your bayonets and get this fellow up.

[Prisoner arises and totters as guards advance.]

SCENE THIRD.

DARK WOOD.

[Enter 1st L. Lucy Johnson and Toney. Lucy Johnson sinks to ground exhausted.]

Toney.—(*Hurriedly*) Oh, Lor', did is orful. Dat mule gin out last night and de poor chile tried to walk. Know'd she could'nt do it no how. Miss Johnson, please look up. (*Lucy turns her head towards him.*) I kin pick yeh up an' tote yeh like a chile, we're near de Yankee lines. Do let me, Miss. De rebels is neah, I seed dem jis down de road afore I com'd up.

Lucy J.—(*Reclining on one arm.*) Toney, God bless you. You have been good and fathful. You did your best. Oh, it is better to die here, wearied and starving under the blue vault of Heaven, than to bear the horrors of imprisonment near that bad man.

Toney.—Let me tote you, Miss. Oh, I kin carry you. (*Starts and looks down the road.*) Afore God, Miss, dere a cumin. Dar, I sees 'em. Dey'll take you again. Let me carry you off.

Lucy J.—Go Toney, save yourself, I feel as if my heart were broken. I cannot live. Go North to Ohio, to Carlton. See my father and tell him how I died. Here (*removes a ring from her finger,*) give this to my father for Louis Ludlow should he live. (*Starts up and looks down the road, then sinks*) Save yourself, Toney. Go, go, they are coming.

Toney.—(*looking down the road.*) Yes, Miss, dey are cumin', but 'fore Heaven dey aint rebels. Dey are near here an' got no guns. De large man is a helpen de odder. He's a 'scapin Yankee. I see dey is near. Don't be skeered,

[Lucy springs to her feet, looks down the road, then gives a cry of joy.]

ENTER 1ST L. LOUIS LUDLOW AND BOB MASON.

Lucy J.—Oh, Louis, Louis, my own Louis. (*Faints in Louis Ludlow's arms.*)

Louis L.—(*To Toney.*) Boy, how is this, explain quick. (*Draws pistol.*)

Toney.—Stop, Massa, I'm Miss Johnson's friend. She went amiss in Tennessee, an' Cap'n Thornton captured her an' took her with Longstreet to Virginia. He was a goin' to have her hung, but I heerd him, an' she's 'scapin wud me now to de Union lines. Dis is true. (*Lucy Johnson recovers*)

Louis L.—My darling Lucy. Did you indeed carry out your plan to go to Tennessee to nurse the wounded.

Lucy J.—I did Louis. I did.

Louis L.—And were you captured by that scoundrel, Thornton, and are you now escaping.

Lucy J.—Yes, Louis, and this brave boy, Toney, has saved me. Thank him, thank him.

Louis L.—(*To Toney.*) Forgive me for my fears. God bless you my brave fellow.

Toney.—Dat's all right. Reckon Miss Lucy 'ill let you tote her all day.

Bob M.—(*Who has been looking to the right.*) The day is breaking. Away off I see the flag an' the fires, and here close at hand are the Union soldiers. Hurrah for Gineral Jackson.

[All cheer as Union pickets enter 1st R. Louis Ludlow hurriedly opens his breast.]

Louis L.—We are escaped prisoners. Here is the flag of my regiment. I was color sergeant. No rebel hand ever touched it. Thank God it is back without disgrace,

Soldiers.—Three cheers for the color guard. Hip, hip, &c.

Louis L.—Here is a lady, I will explain all when I get to camp. Conduct me to your commanding officer.

[ALL EXIT 1ST R.]

SCENE FOURTH.

WOOD OR LANDSCAPE.

[Camp of Federal troops discovered asleep. Guards in rear. Assembly. Troops fall in for roll call. Adjutant reports troops dismissed. Enter pickets 2nd R. escorting Louis Ludlow, Lucy Johnson, Bob Mason and Toney.]

Sergeant.—Escaped prisoners from Richmond. Here is a sergeant who never forsook his colors.

[Louis Ludlow exhibits flag to officer. Lucy Johnson given a seat. Soldiers gather around and cheer.]

SONG.—THE STANDARD WATCH.

Where floats the Standard o'er the tented plain,
His lonely watch the minstrel knight is keeping,
And thus beguiles the time with tuneful strain
His silver lute with mailed finger sweeping.
The lady of my love I may not name,
I dare not hope my love can be requited ;
Yet I will fight for Liberty and fame,
Beneath the banner where my vows were plighted.
Beneath the banner where my vows were plighted.

The night is gone, the battle comes with day :
Behold, the bard surrounding foes defying,
Red carnage marks his presence in the fray,
While still he sings amid the dead and dying.
The lady of my love I may not name,
I dare not hope my love can be requited :
Then let me die for Liberty and fame,
Beneath the banner where my vows were plighted.
Beneath the banner where my vows were plighted.

The fight is won, death sated quits the field :
Yet still the faithful bard, while life is fleeting,
Expiring lies upon his gory shield,
This dying note with feeble voice repeating.
The lady of my love I did not name,
In Heaven above we may yet be united ;
I fought and fell for liberty and fame,
Beneath the banner where my vows were plighted,
Beneath the banner where my vows were plighted.

TABLEAUX.

ACT V.

SCENE FIRST.

Wood or Lanscape. Lapse of Eighteen Months. Music.— Marching through Georgia. A Bivouac of Union troops on the march to the sea. Night scene. Soldiers in groups sitting down. Guards rear. Enter Bummers laden with fowls, meat, &c. Are greeted with laughter and cheers.

Bob. M.—Afore we started on this march from Atlanta. I would have bet a critter to a plug of terbaka, that Jim Browulow's Tennesseeans was the heaviest foragers in the army; but thar's no use talken, you'uns have got a nat'ral knack at foragin' that no 'mount of teachin' I'll give. See heah Sam Roberts what in thunder did yeh bring them ar crinoline heah fur? We can't eat it, an' Uncle Bill Sherman won't let yeh wear it, an' if he did you wouldn't. Its no more use than two tails to a yellar purp.

Sam R.—Now see here Bob, I'll tell yeh why I hankered arter that crinoline. I've got a gal up home, an' as we're a driven fur the sea, I thought it would remind me of Abbey Smith. We ought to have something to remind us of a woman 'bout camp.

Bob M.—I've know'd fellers as lost thar har an' they never scratched thar heads without thinkin' of a woman.

Sam R.—(*Holding up the crinoline.*) Never mind Bob, we can tie up this and can use it for catchin' turkeys.

Bob M.—Wall it may come in play that way for its caught a goose already.

[Louis Ludlow advances laughing at the crinoline.]

Sam R.—See here Louis. Do you think Abbey would wear that if I took it North.

Louis L.—(*laughing.*) Wear it? Yes over your back. But did you hear the news?

Soldiers.—(*Gathering around.*) No.

Louis L.—Well, we are to strike Savannah in a few days. And then we move North for God's country.

Soldiers—Hurrah for God's country.

Louis L.—I think that fight of yesterday was the last. We wiped out Thornton pretty well.

Bob M.—We took all the fight out of him, as the doctors said when they put the chaps head in a kag of fourth proof whisky.

Sam R.—Thunder but I feel good. Lets have a song. Raise her up boys, and I'll come in on the chorus like a forty pound hammer on a nail.

SONG.—*Air.* CHEER BOYS, CHEER.

Cheer boys cheer, we're marching on to battle,
  Cheer boys cheer, for your sweethearts and you wives.
Cheer boys cheer, we'll nobly do our duty,
  And give to the Union, Our hearts, our arms and lives
As onward we march praying for the ending,
  Let us implore a blessing from on high.
Our cause is just, the right from wrong defending,
  And the God of battles will listen to our cry.
    CHORUS—Cheer boys, cheer, &c.

Look up to the sky, the clouds will soon be breaking.
  Look forward at the foe, before us he must yield,
Then throw up the flag, the traitors have forsaken,
  And ring out your battle cry, and forward to the field.
CHO.—Cheer boys, cheer, we're ready for the battle,
  Cheer boys, cheer, for your sweethearts and your wives
  And as around the storm of death may rattle
    We'll give to the Union our hearts, our arms, our lives.

Close up the line, for Liberty is pleading,
  Draw every sword, for Treason we defy.
Forward in the charge, Sherman our troops is leading,
  And the God of battles is bending to our cry.
CHORUS—Cheer boys, cheer, &c.

Sam R.—That's a good song, but you ought to hear the one I composed about Abbey. I writ it down at Kenesaw mountain, one evenin' when I was feeling skeered and did'nt expect to see her no more.

Soldiers—Sing it Sam. Lift her up.

Sam R.—No boys. If I was to sing that sad song you'd all get cryin' so the waters would rise, an' we could'nt git out of camp without a pontoon.

Bob M.—I heard a very sorry sounden song one of our East Tennessee gals writ to one of Jim Brownlow's men. I can't sing any mor'n a cat kin blow a horn, but some of the words is:

'Tis hard for you uns to go to war,
  Tis hard for you uns to fight.

4

'Tis hard for you uns to march all day
   An' sleep in a tent at night.
But 'tis harder for we'uns from you'ns to part
Whin you'uns have got we'unses heart. (*Laughter.*)

Now I call that poetry, only Jim's fellows don't sleep in any tents much.

[Laughter heard to rear of camp. Enter Tom Flynn looking very much exhausted,]

Louis L.—Hello, where did you come from Tom. Did you drop from the clouds, or spring from the ground.

Tom F.—Nayther, Mr. Ludlow. Och, luck at me. Its mesel's the sorry looken Tom Flynn, an' if it was'nt that I've given up whiskey I'd be the dhryest one of me family since the flood.

Louis L.—But tell me, where did you come from?

Tom F.—Shure ye might better ax me where I did'nt come from. Fur three years I've been moven night and day, with my body growin shlender, an me pay growin less, till I just axed mesel, Tom Flynn, whats all this fighten an fasten for? Shure the Yankees wuz always me friens an they never hurt a chick or a chile of mine. Well yisterday Captain Thornton was killed.

Louis L.—(*in surprise*) Thornton killed!

Tom F.—Yes, begorra, dead as a nail. I dont know but some how that man bewitched me, though I knowed all the time he wasnt good. Well lasht night to the shame of mesel be it said I desarted, and got into the Yankee pickets. They took me to the Ginral and divil a one of me knowed which ind I was standin on while he talked. When he wuz dun I sid Ginral might I make bould to ax yer name. Of coorse ye may siz he, me name is Sherman. Sherman says I, looken at an impty bottle would a glass near it on the table. If your name is Sherman thin God help Wade Hampton. Well he sint me out an I axed the officer as a great favor to come down to see you. He laughed and sint a man would watch me. Though its mesel's as inocent as a lamb from this day an'—

Louis L.—Well, Tom, you need some better clothes. I will try to get you some.

Tom F.—Very thrue for ye, Mr. Ludlow, my outside lucks bad of coorse, but if ye could se my inside it'ed frighten ye shure enough.

Louis L.—I have no doubt such an exhibition would alarm me.

Tom F.—Och my intestines are in a state of surprise. Not a bit nor a sup has crossed me lips, barren wather, since yistherday.

Louis L.—Well, go back there, the boys will take care of you.

Bob M.—That feller dont mean bad in good company, [*Exit Tom Flynn*] but I would'nt like to trust him in a room whar thar wuz only one drink of whiskey, an nobody looken at it.

Louis L.—Poor fellow if he gets back to Carlton I will help him. Our midnight march will soon begin. Pack up there men.

[Assembly sounds, regiments form hurriedly but in order, men equipped like veterans, order given and troops move forward. Music—*Marching through Georgia.*]

SCENE SECOND.

STREET SCENE IN WASHINGTON.

Bob M.—[ENTER 1ST R.] Wall, this is Washington. Dogon'd if I ever seed sich a place in my life. Wonder why in thunder they made sich a fuss 'bout not lettin the rebels take it. I swar, I think it 'ed a done the place right smart good to have the Johnnies run through it. They allers created a healthy sintament wherever they went. I'll say that for them, now that they are all gin up. [Neatly dressed officer passes.] Wall now, thars suthin shiney. I'll bet a critter that ar chap's a kernel or suthin an never smelled powder durin the war. 'Pears like thars piles of sich varmin in this town. I wouldn't be that chap for all his shiney clothes. Thunder! I'd rather be Bob Mason, who wore a blouse an' carried a gun, and did his whole duty whin thar was guns a rattlin', than one of them peace Ginerals an officers, who felt big at a table with pens ahind thar ears, an little orderlies to run like rabbits at their order. [A highly dressed colored woman passes.] Thunder an lightnin, ain't that stunnin. Don't that ar jest take down everything I ever seed. Wonder if them's her Sunday clothes. Wall, I reckoned on that after the 'mancipation. Why thar ain't a gal in East Tennessee kin begin to come nigh that ar Queen of Shebar. Wonder if that pusson wants to hire a waiter? Wall, if she does, she would'nt hev me; I can't wait wuth a cuss. Thar, I'll go down this street, Pennsylvania avenue I think they calls it. But them chaps at the close stores I reckon thinks I'm naked, the way they goes for me. What powerful winnin ways they has. No, I won't go down that street. I'd have to buy some clothes if them little cusses run at me agin.

Enter News Boy.—Star, sir. Intelligise. Chronikal. Black yer boots sir, shine em up sir, army shine, Capting,

Bob M.—See heah, yeh sopy little catamount! ain't you got no mother to mend your pants?

News Boy.—No sir, never had none.

Bob M.—Poor little cuss. I don't want your papers nor boots blacked. Heah's a four levy bit.

News Boy—[Running off.] Thank you, boss.

Bob M.—[*Calling him back.*] See heah, get them pants o' youru reinforced. Heah's ten cents. Go down pass that clothing shop whar that feller stan's watchin' at the door, and bring me some chawin' terbacker.

News Boy.—All right, sir. [EXIT.]

Bob M.—Poor little cuss, he'll be ruined if he grows up in this place with all them Congressmen an' sich.

[ENTER MR. LUDLOW.]

Mr. Ludlow.—Ah, my friend, I am glad to see the soldiers home again. Are you one of Sherman's men?

Bob M.—Yes, sir. I helped tote Uncle Billy round heah. Our folks is across the river neah that thunderin' long bridge. We'uns is waitin' to show off in—review, I think they calls it, (*looking down the street*). What keeps that little varmint with the terbacker.

Mr. L.—I have just come on from Ohio, to see the review. I have two sons who are with Sherman, and I hope to take them home with me.

Bob M.—Thunder you say! Two sons a bummin' with us down in Georgia! Stranger, heah's my han'. Yer the fust pure white man I've seed in this town. What in thunder keeps that little cuss with the terbacker!

Mr. L.—Pardon me, but did you send a boy for tobacco?

Bob M.—Yes, a little thing what aint got no mother, come along a wanten to sell me papers and black my boots. A ragged little cuss. I gave him four bits for himself, and ten cents to get me some terbacker. 'Reckon them clothes shop men, seein' his raggedness, have gone for him. They jest went for me.

Mr. L.—Those are bad boys. I fear this one will not return with the tobacco.

Bob M.—The thunder you say! Wall, if that little varmint don't come back, an' I see him again, his pants will need half-solin' wuss than now.

Mr. L.—Perhaps you knew my sons in the service. One was named Louis, and the other Jackson Ludlow?

Bob M.—What, say that agin. You the father of Louis Ludlow?

Mr. L.—Louis, the color bearer, for whom I now have a commission as captain, is my son.

Bob M.—Hurrah! Your hand. Both on 'em. Thar. By Thunder I'm glad ter see you. My name's Bob Mason. Oh, Gineral Jackson, but I'm glad to meet you.

Mr. L.—(*Heartily*) No more glad than I am to meet you. My sons write about you every week, and I feel towards you like a brother. God bless you, Bob Mason. (*Again shaking his hand.*)

Bob M.—Come, let us leave this place and go to camp. We'll take care of you. We'll show you the colors, an' the color guard 'll just put you through or I aint Bob Mason.

Mr. L.—I was just going to camp, having received a special permit. Promise me you will go home with me when mustered out.

Bob M.—Of course I will. Wait till this dogon'd review is over. (*As they walk off Bob looks back and says,*) I swear I'd give ten dollahs to lay my hand on that onery little cuss what has my terbacker.

SCENE THIRD.

SCENE IN THE VILLAGE OF CARLTON.

[Squire Williams and Farmer Johnson discovered.]

Squire W.—Well, Mr. Johnson we have crushed down this rebellion at last. I knew we would do it. I did my level best. Susan Maria ain't a widder to be sure, but Jim Hansom tried hard to be killed. He's still on crutches.

Farmer J.—Never mind your own bold exploits now, Squire. We must talk of nobler men. You know the boys are coming back to-day. The train will soon be in, and we have a welcome for them.

[ENTER TOM FLYNN AND VILLAGERS]

Tom F.—Good morrow, Misther Johnson.

Farmer J.—Good morning. Tom. How do you like hard work?

Tom F.—Loike hard work! Shure its mesel was raised to it. I never felt betther in my life. I never let a dhrop of whisky touch me lips. But on course to-day, wud Captain Ludlow cumin home, it would not be dacent not to dhrink his health. Barren that divil a one of me we'll ever become a shlave to the nasty stuff again.

[ENTER JERUSHA JOHNSON, ALICE GRAY AND ABBIE SMITH.]

Jerusha J.—[To Farmer Johnson.] Well, I'm glad it's all over. Who'd a thought Mr. Goodman would have married a hospital nurse? Oh, this war has ruined so many good men.

Abbey S.—Miss Gurusha, I'm agoin to leave you after Captain Ludlow marries Miss Lucy.

Jerusha J.—Why what will become of you? Where are you going?

Abbey S.—Nowhere's. Sam and me is goin to start a blacksmith shop together.

Alice G.—There they are coming. Glory, the boys are back, and Jack will be all the handsomer with his one arm.

[Music. "Hail to the Chief." Troops march on with colors. Enter Mr. Ludlow and Lucy Johnson. The soldiers break ranks to exchange greetings for a few moments, then tne assembly sounds and the troops form with colors centre; Jack Johnson carrying them with his remaining arm.]

Louis L.—(Commands) colors to the front. Miss Johnson—four years ago I received from the ladies of this place, through you, a beautiful flag, the emblem of our united country. War was then upon us, and as I accepted the colors I promised that in our hands they should never receive a stain. Since then we have borne them on the march, in the battle, through the prison pens of the South, and with Sherman to the Sea, and north to the capitol of the land we helped to save. Here I return them battered, blood stained and faded, but brighter with glory than they were before.

Lucy J.—Captain Ludlow, in the name of the ladies of Carlton, I receive the flag so indicative of the valor of the Color Guard, to whom we entrusted it. Henceforth it will be a sacred legacy, which he shall hand down to coming generations, to remind them of the heroism that kept our land united and to warn them should ambition lead them to raise their hands against the flag.

[While the ladies in wonder examine the flag in Lucy's hand, the order is given.] Presant Arms! Carry Arms! Order Arms! Stack Arms! Attention! Regiment free. Break ranks. March.

Mr. L.—(*Shaking hands with Bob Mason.*) Let me welcome you, here Mr. Mason, and urge upon you to come work and live with us.

Bob M.—I'm right glad to be heah, and will often come up to see yeh; but I would not live away from the mountains and rivers of East Tennessee. To whom is the sky so blue, the air so clear, an' the hills so grand. Thar's whar is sleepin' all who had my blood in thar vains, an' her I loved. I'll go back an' hang up my rifle an' take to plowin' the valleys, an' when I grows rich, you'ns must come an' see me an' stay all the time.

Louis L.—Well, Bob, I'm glad it's all over. Now I am going to marry and settle down, and only talk of war when I meet an old comrade like you.

Sam R.—I'm glad I didn't bring that crinoline home from Georgia. Abbey says she's got new ones. The gal's been preparin' for the weddin' for a long time. Captain, you've got to do it fust.

Jack J.—(*who has been talking to Alice Gray.*) See here, Louis, you remember those socks I got down in Tennessee, with a note in them!

Louis L.—(*Smiling.*) Yes, very well.

Jack J.—I thought at the time, that aunt Jerusha wrote that note, hoping it would fall into Mr. Goodman's hands, but it appears this child sent it. It has a better effect than if any one else had done it.

Alice G.—I wish I could have gone South with Lucy.

Toney.—Wall, Miss, I'm glad yeh didn't. This chile had a hard job keerin' for one young lady. Don't know what he'd a gone dun if thar was two.

Fanny G.—Jack, my boy, I'm more than glad to see you back. You have lost an arm. But you are more of a man than ever. I am glad I had a boy to fight for the flag.

Tom F.—Yis an if all the marriges takes place, I think there will, by me sowl there'll soon be plenty more boys in Carlton to fight for the flag.

Louis L.—Yes, my friends, I hope henceforth for peace and prosperity in the free South and a united land. But should danger threaten the old flag again it will not want for a Color Guard to defend it.

Music. *Hail Columbia.*

TABLEAUX. Union, Freedom. Prosperity.

www.ingramcontent.com/pod-product-compliance
Lightning Source LLC
Chambersburg PA
CBHW022207020726
47496CB00008B/2913